Thanksgiving

written by
Karen Evans
Kathleen Urmston

illustrated by
Dennis Graves

November is here.

Soon we will go to Grandma's house.

We made pictures
of Indians at
school today.

Soon we will go to
Grandma's house.

Mom put a turkey and
a pilgrim in our window

Soon we will go to Grandma's house.

Mom baked pumpkin
pies today.

Tomorrow we will go
to Grandma's house.

"Put on your coats," said Dad. "We are going to Grandma's house."

M-m-m-m!
It smells so good
at Grandma's house.

It's Thanksgiving Day!